Level 4   Book 3

words
s t o r i e s

Snow White and the Seven Dwarves

Stories adapted by Shirley Jackson
Illustrated by Sue Reeves of Advocate
Series designed by Jeannette Slater

Copyright © 2000 Egmont World Limited, a division of Egmont Holding Limited.
All rights reserved.
Published in Great Britain by Egmont World Limited, Deanway Technology Centre,
Wilmslow Road, Handforth, Cheshire SK9 3FB
Printed in Germany
ISBN 0 7498 4659 3
A CIP catalogue record for this book is available from the British Library

poisoned apple

magic cloak

glass coffin

Snow White

magic mirror

deer

heart

wicked stepmother

huntsman

Once upon a time, there was a beautiful princess.

She was called Snow White.

Snow White had a wicked stepmother, the queen.

o new words

The queen liked to look in her magic mirror.

Every day, she asked, "Mirror, mirror, on the wall, who is the fairest of them all?"

Every day, the magic mirror said, "You are the fairest of them all."

new words **asked** **wall** **fairest** **them**

Snow White grew into a beautiful woman.

One day, the queen asked, "Mirror, mirror, on the wall, who is the fairest of them all?"

The magic mirror said, "Snow White is the fairest of them all."

The queen called for her huntsman.

"Go to the forest and kill Snow White," she said coldly. "I want her heart."

But the huntsman could not kill Snow White.

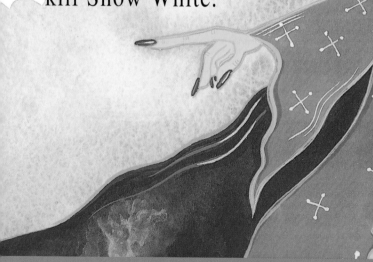

new words   **kill   coldly**

"Run away," he said, "and
do not come back – ever."
Snow White ran and ran.

The huntsman killed a deer.
He gave the deer's heart to
the queen.

Snow White found a
little house.

She knocked on the door,
but there was no answer.

When Snow White went inside,
she saw seven little chairs.

She saw seven little beds.

Snow White went to sleep
on the seven little beds.

When Snow White woke up,
she saw seven little men.

She told them the story about
the queen and the huntsman
and the deer.

"You can live here," said
the seven little men.
"We will look after you."

Back at the castle, the queen asked her magic mirror, "Mirror, mirror, on the wall, who is the fairest of them all?"

"Snow White is the fairest of them all," came the answer.

The queen saw the little house in the magic mirror.

no new words

The queen put on her magic cloak. She looked like an old woman.

The queen went to the little house and knocked at the door.

Snow White saw a kind, old woman and let her come in.

But the kind, old woman gave Snow White a poisoned apple.

Snow White took one bite of the poisoned apple and fell to the floor.

new words   **bite**   **floor**

Back at the castle, the
wicked queen asked her
magic mirror,
"Mirror, mirror, on the wall,
who is the fairest of
them all?"

"You are the fairest of
them all," came the answer.

The queen was happy.

no new words

The little men found
Snow White.

They put her in a glass coffin.

Snow White was in a deep,
deep sleep.

The little men were very sad.

Every day, they waited by
the coffin.

One day, a prince saw
Snow White and fell in love
with her.

He gave Snow White a
magic kiss.

Snow White woke up.

Snow White and the prince
married and lived happily
ever after.